To Niamh,
a true Christmas star

First published 2003 by
Walker Books Ltd. 87 Vauxhall Walk
London SE11 5HJ

10 9 8 7 6 5 4 3 2 1

© 2003 Mary Murphy

The right of Mary Murphy to be identified as the
author-illustrator of this work has been asserted by
her in accordance with the Copyright, Designs
and Patents Act 1988

This book has been typeset in M Murphy One

Printed in Singapore

British Library Cataloguing in Publication Data:
a catalogue record for this book is available
from the British Library

ISBN 0-7445-8802-2 (hb)
ISBN 1-84428-450-6 (pb)

Little Owl and the Star

a Christmas story by Mary Murphy

WALKER BOOKS
AND SUBSIDIARIES
LONDON · BOSTON · SYDNEY

It was a silent night.

I sat in my tree,
with a waiting
feeling.

A star sparkled along.
"Follow me, Little Owl!"
said the star.

And I did.

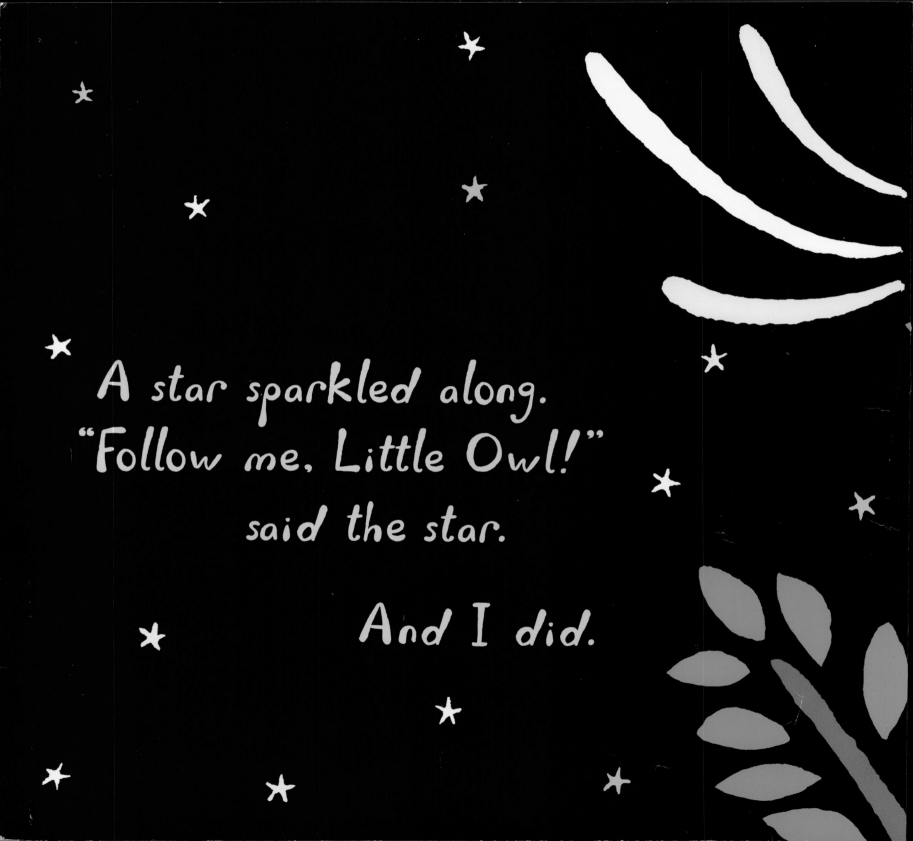

We saw three camels, plodding softly through sand.

There were men with them, watching the sky.

"Follow us," said the star.
And they did.

"Follow us," said the star.
And they did.

On we flew.
We heard singing,
a song of great joy.

"Who is that singing?"
I asked.

"Angels,"
said the star.
"Oh," I said.
"Aren't they lovely!"

Then we stopped, over a stable.
"I'll stay in the sky,
Little Owl," said the star.
"But you look in the stable."

So I did.

The stable was warm and quiet.
I saw a donkey and a cow,
and a man and a woman.

They were looking at a baby,
sleeping in a manger.

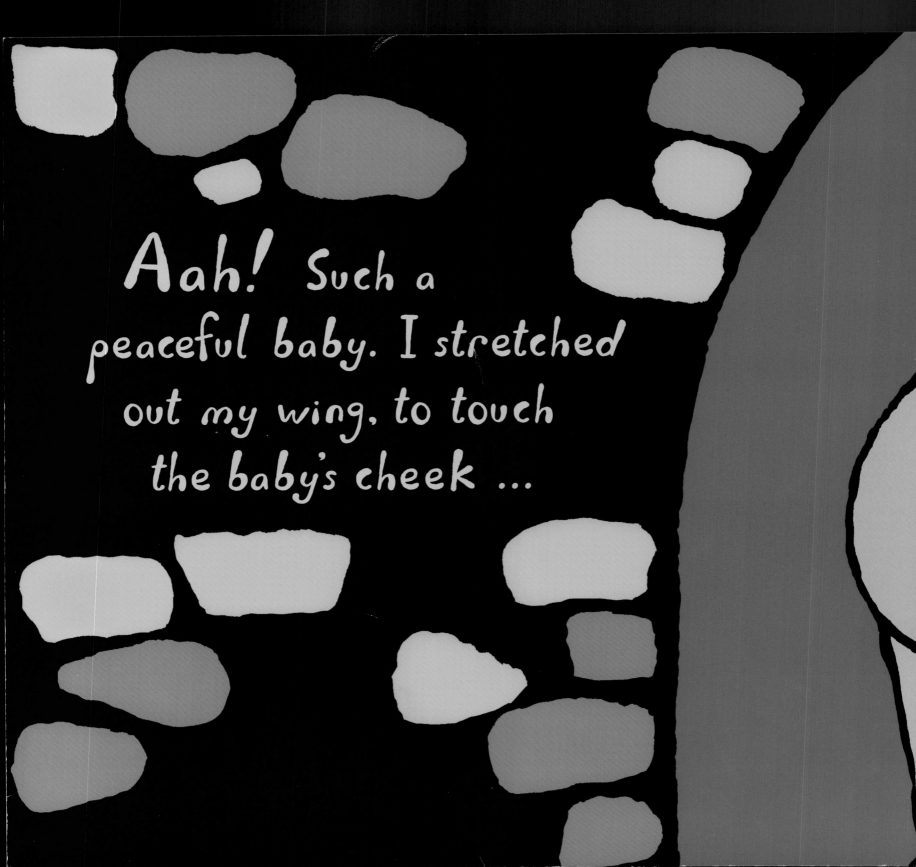

Aah! Such a peaceful baby. I stretched out my wing, to touch the baby's cheek ...

and the baby woke and smiled.
What a happy smile!

The smile went right inside me.
The waiting feeling went away.

Then everyone came: the sheep and the shepherds, the camels and the travelling men. The baby smiled and waved, and everyone smiled back.

I flew back to the star.

"What a happy,
      happy baby!" I said.

The star shone very bright,
and filled the world
      with light.